BAKER STREET

UNIVERSE TALES

SEVEN

John Pirillo

Copyright 2022

BEAST OF THE NORTH FORK MOORS

Deadly Intent, Deadly Purpose

Several days ago.

He hadn't meant to disturb the order of things.

But he had.

Now he must pay.

He darted his eyes right and left as he crept through the tall rushes that hid the brackish waters and what hid beneath them.

Hunting him now.

Hunting him for days.

He could barely breathe; his lungs ached so badly from the strain of his terror. Of his flight to evade deadly intent and the purpose, he had discovered.

Creak.

What was that?

The moon was high overhead and the shadows gathered about him, like lurking monsters, ready at any given moment to leap forward and sweep him beneath the waters to his death.

While there was generally nothing to fear in the waters...this was night. He knew what glided barely beneath the surface of the rough waters, its nose barely poking above the waters as it wiggled its deadly shape forward.

They were known as five-step snakes.

One.

Two.

Three.

Four.

Five.

You were dead.

That fast.

The soft bottom of the moor suddenly gave way.

He tried to scream.

But he could not.

His mouth filled with the horrible-tasting liquid as he sank into its murky depths.

221B Baker Street

Several days later.

"What I wouldn't give for a few nice days out in the country," Ms. Hudson sighed.

"With my luck, I'd step into a pothole and drown."

She laughed. "John, you big silly. You wouldn't even fit into a pothole."

He laughed. "Not as long as the woman I love keeps me well fed, I should hope not."

"But I'm serious."

"So am I," Watson replied. He glanced from the fireplace, seated on a comfortable chair, the morning London Times in his lap.

"I hate the countryside. Too many crawling, flying things that get into your shoes, crawl up your legs and into your mouth."

Ms. Hudson, standing next to the fireplace, turned about and smacked Watson on the side of his head. But lightly.

He grinned.

"John, stop teasing me!"

"I'm not. I thoroughly detest the outdoors."

She sighed. "That's because you and Sherlock are always tramping off somewhere having a party of an adventure."

He gave her a good-natured smile. "My dear, your idea of a party does not fit vampires, werewolves, demons, switchblade ghouls, and the sorts we encounter at all."

She put her arms around his neck and nuzzled him, breathing against his ear. "Think of all the fun things we could do there."

Watson's eyes lit up.

Run!

Several days ago.

He burst free from the murky waters, spitting out the grime and slime that had flooded his throat.

He gagged for several long moments, throwing up the vile taste from his upset stomach.

He stood there, safely once more on the solid bottom, his eyes burning, throat aching, lungs aching for more air.

He had stood too long.

A shadow fell across him.

He didn't bother to turn around.

To look back.

He knew what was following him.

His only thought was to run.

Fast.

Faster.

Don't look back.

Keep running.

His lungs felt like they were about to burst.

He heard it gaining on him.

It was inhumanly fast.

He had so little energy left.

He could feel the muscles in his legs burning as if they were on fire.

His lungs were on fire.

His forehead was dripping sweat like a waterfall. And it was winter.

He only had a bit more to go and he would be safe.

Surely they wouldn't follow him there.

He saw the path in the falling light of day and veered in that direction, his arms wind-milling as he forced himself to do so.

The path declined swiftly to the usually golden moor below, which now seemed to be a lake of fire as the descending sun cast its red and gold rays across the reeds and cat's tails that sprayed the length and breadth of it.

Only a few more feet.

For some strange reason, he couldn't hear it following him anymore. The heavy footfalls were missing.

He didn't take any chance. Not now when safety, and freedom were so close.

He practically dove into the water, grateful for the immediate cold wash of it upon his skin as he strove to get deeper and deeper.

Finally, he was about ten yards from the shore.

Nothing like that could follow him in here. It was too big. Too heavy.

He bent over, gasping for air, his breath rattling painfully in his lungs.

Slowly his breathing became more even.

He stood up straight and smiled

"I've done it!" He dared to admit to the setting sun behind him. "I've done it!" He uttered once more, tears of relief streaking his face.

Then he felt two enormous hands grab his shoulders and twist him around so he was facing his greatest fear. The terror that had been following him. Almost as if purposely intending him to panic, to rush where he shouldn't, to lose control of his senses.

It had worked.

He would have screamed were he able.

But he was pulled beneath the waters before he could even blink.

221B Baker Street

Several days later.

Holmes came up the stairs into the sitting room at a rapid pace. He swung his arms upwards, and then bent over, then up and over.

He repeated it several times, and then lifted his right leg, set it down, then the left. Repeated that.

He rolled his hips in a circle, then his neck back and forth, causing the vertebrae to make crackling sounds.

"I so hate that sound, Holmes," Watson told him, setting his paper down to watch Holmes finish his exercises.

Holmes smiled. "You should try them. You'd feel so much better."

Watson shook his head vigorously. "Ms. Hudson would never approve of it."

"Says who?" Ms. Hudson inquired, coming behind Holmes. She stood up and gave him a light kiss on his right cheek, then headed for the table with a silver tray with beautiful red roses on all four corners. It was heaped with scones and coffee cups and a steaming pot.

Holmes eyed it. "Well, maybe we can discuss this after breakfast."

Watson jumped up and hurried to the table. "With that, I heartily agree."

As they both sat down, a pounding came from the front door.

Watson rolled his eyes.

Ms. Hudson gave him a warning glance and he bit back his words, but as soon as she descended from view to see to the door, he said, "Constable Evans, no doubt, with a new mission of urgency."

"Then you'd best hurry up and eat, hadn't you, Watson?" Holmes suggested with the hint of a smile.

"Good idea, Holmes."

Watson helped himself to a scone.

The Hollow Path

A day ago.

To say that he was a poor man was just as easy to say as he was a rich man. A man wealthy far beyond most men's dreams. He was both this and that, but he was above all a good person of untarnished character. Joseph Martin was a man who loved nature above all else and even though he had no physical wealth to flaunt like a flag to show his character, he had something far greater in the minds of his friends. He had a character of great disposition that was capable of rousing people to great heights of emotion. It was a tool he used often. It was an enabler and a method for him to do what he loved best. But more importantly, he had a heart of gold and so standing at the fringe of the moors, the skies goldening his view from edge to edge, made him feel like an ancient god amid an Empire of Splendor.

And why shouldn't he be proud and feel like that? Just look at all the browns and golden hues spreading like Midas gold across the entire view. It was magnificent and filled him with awe. The awe of a world that was sometimes blackened by man's indecency to the very world that nurtured him.

He sighed. The weight of his position weighed down on him momentarily.

Also concerns.

He had come out this day for the usual, but also because of growing rumors. Some tourists who had come here of late were leaving early, complaining that something odd was going on. Or that they had seen something unexplainable. Something frightening.

He had laughed it off. People always see something when they're alone in the wilderness. That's when the entire childish fears crop together to overwhelm our imaginations as they once did in our youth.

He smiled.

But then...

Here, he frowned deeply. Here might be things not normally seen, even in the wilds of other parts of the Britains. This land, so large and spread across so many miles, had many areas which were still unexplored. The government didn't have the time or the inclination to pay for more than such as he to preserve the wilderness gathered so beautifully before him.

Protect the North York Moors!

That was the motto posted at the entrance to the park. And rightly so.

Modern land developers were looking in this direction a lot of late as they planned for future and more ambitious projects. Called communities. They would be building specialized communities for the middle rich. The people who were not wealthy wanted more than just a flat in London.

Life was getting too dangerous and too complex in the big city. He knew that, but he didn't have to like it. So the developers were eyeing spots like his; eyeing it with the idea of buying it and turning it into gold. True Midas gold, not just the splendor of nature.

And then this area would one day be gone. Lost like so many areas that had been wilderness at one time and were now filled with soot and ash, toxic chemicals, and angry renters, because of the money they had to pay out just to have a roof over their heads.

He sighed again.

Sometimes he wondered if civilization wasn't coming to an end finally. What the dark magicians and wizards and barbarians of the North hadn't destroyed through war and poisoning, the developers would with their greed for money.

But…this…he eyed the golds and hues about him once more, the brackish moor waters that ebbed and flowed like a living thing, the golden straw-like reeds that thrust proudly from the mud below the water and into the air, the somewhat ancient trees that leaned sadly, but sternly amongst the growth, this was his life's ambition and what he considered worthy of doing beyond all else. He wanted his children, his children's children, and all future generations to see what he saw now: A vast array of Mother Nature's magical kingdom ranging from the tiniest of insects with gossamer wings that buzzed from tilting flower mouths to tilted flower mouth, to the vaster denizens who hid in the water and grasses, shrubs and trees, keeping to themselves, harming none. Creatures of ancient beauty and majestic stature.

Some are as old as time itself.

He never spoke of those sightings.

He didn't even know if anyone else was aware of them. But he knew they lived here in one of the last sanctuaries for the magical life that was once abundant and reaching out into all areas of the Britains. It was their last fortress against the maddening civilization that threatened to consume and spit out the planet.

Here there be gods of life, not of man. He thought to himself. And he trusted those gods more than the gods of man that blessed and encouraged war of man against man.

An Emperor Moth spread its golden wings, taking to flight as a pair of Snipes, their sharp wings arrowing the sky disturbing the nest of rushes they had been hiding within. An owl hooted further back on one of the low-hanging maples that draped the lower part of the moors. He could see its glistening brown eyes, his reflection looking back at him. He had a marvelous vision at his age and he thanked God for it every day, as it allowed the enrichment of his soul with the beauty of and the bounty of the almost endless moors that stretched like a sleeping giant of yore all about him.

The Emperor Moth gathered his court as he flew, and soon he was trailed by dozens of the huge things, and then pursued by the Snipes, Sparrows, and Pigeons that were waiting for just this opportunity.

The cycle of life. He smiled to himself. One eats. One is eaten. No anger. No remorse. No greed. No regret. Just a quick shuffling of balances. Life to death. Death to life.

The dozens of moths that were eaten would supply the birds that ate them with nourishment, which in turn would seed the moors and moors with further eggs and seeds that would grow into more moths, plants, and flowers. An endless cycle of a glorious life!

Joe, as his colleagues called him, was a New Age adventurer. The fanciful name New Age was something that Jules Verne had coined after one of his and his friend Wells's long journeys through time. A coin that he loved being able to spend. And did frequently, along with the Good Queen Mary of Scots, who was an ardent supporter of the ecology and the maintaining it for future generations.

New Age. It sounded so fresh and exciting he began to bill himself as the New Age Philosopher. A Philosophy of New Age Planetary Proportions became the founding name of a society he created. It was attended more and more by wealthy men of stature, as well as learned men from the highest institutions on the planet. Its sole purpose was to preserve known creatures and the ones not so known yet. Some that others might even call mythical were they to come out into the light of day. They were also protected if that need should ever surface.

He was well-liked by every man he had met so far, except for one obnoxious fellow who kept pretending his life was in danger. Finally, he told the man to take his leave and never to return to any of the meetings. He regretted being so harsh, but the man was getting on his nerves. Why would anyone want to kill him for wanting to protect the beauty of the Moors? He had told his best friend and fellow adventurer, Sir Ellison of the potential threat and he had laughed it off as well.

But when he told his wife, she had turned as pale as a ghost and run into her bedroom, locking the door. No manner of besieging could get her out to speak with him. The next morning it was as if nothing whatsoever had happened.

She gave him his usual breakfast of ham and eggs, fresh bread heaped with warm butter and fresh marmalade, and then he helped with the dishes. He would put on his coat and hat, she would give him the usual war kiss he always looked forward to, and then he went to work once more, thinking all was right in his world. And it was!

But at the back of his mind was what his wife had done the night before. She had said no more about it, but he knew it was still bothering her because she burned both the ham and the eggs and the bread was overly buttered and soggy.

He hadn't said anything, not wanting to stir up anything more than it already had been.

Still, he had to admit; perhaps she had the right of it. She wasn't one to jump to conclusions. She was, for all intents and purposes, the more balanced of the two of them. She had feared what he had not. Was he being arrogant? Was he flaunting his moth wings that some future predator might devour if he was not careful?

He stopped a moment at the edge of a patch of thick water brush and lilies that thrust their red throats up into the glorious golden skies of dawn, thirsting for the light that nourished them.

He was wearing his moor boots as he named them. They came up to the top of his trousers. While a bit difficult to navigate in they kept him dry and allowed him to ply the moor waters safely without getting himself sick.

He smiled at the lilies before him and kissed one with the tip of his right forefinger.

If lilies could smile, then this one might have. He could feel its life force beaming up at him. He truly did love it.

He also mused, on the other hand, how *easy their lives are.*

Zip!

Waterfowl flew over his head, calling out to each other as they flapped their lazy gray wings in the dawn light, their eyes blazing orange and red as they glanced back at him a moment. Though for some reason perhaps on the subconscious level, that frightened him, he never could have adequately described to anyone any rational reason why he should feel that way.

He shrugged his shoulders, hefted his waterproof bag from his left shoulder to the right, and his net from the left to the right hand, and began slogging through the moors waters that fed into the moor and kept it fresh and lively, green throughout the year.

He had traced the waters once and found them to be coming from a hidden spring that had been dug out probably ages ago. He had found the remnants of some very oddly structured stone and wood, but gave it no more thought. He had friends at the museum who could find the amusement in his find he did not. He had told them of it, but the dears had to wait for funding as all who worked for the blasted government.

God knew the Good Queen Mary of Scots was the best, but she had a tight fist when it came to projects like that of his friends, preferring to let history be, rather than pursue its roots. So it was no surprise to him now that many months had gone by that the source of the water remained unexplored, as well as quite mysterious.

No matter in the long run. The water fed the moor and that's all that truly mattered.

He paused as he neared the patch of the moors where it became thick with mud and dangerous. He had to tread carefully. He had created a safe path over the months by shoving sticks into the safe areas. Sticks were painted white at the top so they wouldn't be missed.

It was starting to get late now and he had just a bit more of daylight before he ought to hurry out of the moors area and back onto solid land.

He noted the first of the sticks and smiled. He was safely on course.

He went to the second, and then the third angling to the right. He paused a moment. Something was eating at the edge of his mind, but he couldn't think of what it might be. He kept following the sticks and though he was on the right path the sun began to move in front of him and blind him. He shielded his eyes. He smiled. He had gotten slightly off the path.

He laughed at his clumsiness. Keeping his eyes shielded with his hand, he neglected to press the depth pole into the mud as he was wont to do when he came into the boggy portions of the moor because sometimes the bog holes moved around. He didn't know why. They just did.

He reached the next pole safely and then launched himself towards the last. But the shore of the moors seemed further than it should be. He frowned. When he lifted his right foot it was very difficult.

No matter he thought again.

He pulled it free and convinced he was moving towards the solid ground again, he slogged on, splashing mud and dirty water as high as his mud shirt. Then he stuck. He pulled on his stuck right foot. But it wouldn't budge. He pried up his left to set it on more solid ground, but then the ground moved away from him as if it had a life of its own.

He panicked then. This wasn't possible. He was on safe ground, wasn't he?

Desperately he turned about as best he could to search for a lone fisherman who was tempted to fish this time of day. Usually, there were two or three, but for some reason on this day, there were none in sight.

Then he noticed something else. The weeds about him were taller than they had been. No. Wait. That was impossible! He screamed to himself inwardly.

He dropped his net and thrust his staff downwards, searching for solid ground. Nothing. Nothing. Nothing.

Nothing!

The weeds were now a good two feet taller than him. He looked down again. The water was up to his waist.

Then he felt the ground move under him again.

The ground was moving away from him.

221 B Baker Street

Holmes rose to shake Constable Evans's hand, and clap him on the shoulder. "Please, sit with us and have something warm and tasty, I'm sure Watson won't mind."

Constable Evans eyed the remaining scones.

Watson went to grab them and Ms. Hudson chose that moment to hug him. Her eyes were on Constable Evans. She grinned.

He got it.

He hurriedly sat down and took the last two scones onto a fresh plate.

Holmes poured him some coffee.

"Milk?"

"No, this time of day I prefer black."

Holmes nodded. He took his black day or night."

Ms. Hudson let go of Watson. "What was that all about?"

She smiled. "I just love you so much."

Watson gave her a suspicious look and then realized the scones were gone.

She laughed. Pinched his cheek. "My little grumbly

bear misses his scones?"

"I am not…"

She put a scone into his mouth.

That shut him up.

"So, Constable, to what do we owe the honor of this morning's visit?"

Constable Evans wolfed down the remainder of his last scone and then shook his head. "I hate to bring such bad news so early in the morning."

Watson snorted. "Yes, and I like breathing air, so out with it!"

Constable Evans sighed. " Two…"

Watery Grave

A day ago.

No, he was sinking into it.

Somehow he had misread the sticks. He was in the dangerous part of the boggy mud of the moors. He was sinking, slowly, but steadily.

He strove to climb out of his shoes to try and swim away to safety.

He couldn't get out of them. He had never planned on being able to do that and now they were tied tightly about his legs.

He fumbled with the rope cinching the boots on him, but too late.

He was already up to his neck in the brackish water.

He dipped his head down into the water, the better to see the knots holding his legs and feet into his moor boots.

He ran out of air trying to loosen them, just as he was about to free himself.

He raised his head to get more air, but his head didn't break the surface.

He screamed.

Screamed.

No one heard!

How could they?

His screams were beneath the water now. Sending up huge bubbles of air. His last air.

Still, he kept going down.

Something had his boots and was holding them down and pulling him down deeper.

What?

The mud?

Something else?

His last air burst from his lungs and water rushed into them instead.

As he began to black out from lack of oxygen, something moved close by. Something large. Very, very large.

In the last bit of effort to gain help, he flung his hands above the surface of the water, but whatever it was pulled him deeper and his hands barely grazed the surface of the moor.

Above the waters a last stream of bubbles burst into the air, disturbing the waters strongly for a moment, and then there were fewer.

Less.

Then none.

The two water fowl that had flown past earlier flew past again. They let loose forlorn cries, filling the air with a desolate cry.

Another cry joined theirs.

But it was not human.

Holiday in the Country

"What a marvelous idea you had, Holmes."

Holmes turned askew a moment to eye Watson, who had his right hand out the passenger side window and was allowing the wind of their passage to bob his hand up and down as a small child might. He smiled, and then fixed his attention on the road again.

They were traveling a lesser route along a road that wound about the slopes of one of the taller mountains in Switzerland. They were heading for a well-earned rest in the Chateau that Challenger owned. He was going to meet them there.

Watson glanced at the side that Holmes drove upon and noted the huge drop-off on that side. "How high are we anyway?"

"You don't want to know."

"No. I guess I don't," Watson agreed. He didn't tell Holmes that he had been pretending to be comfortable the whole time they ascended when in fact he was shaken to the very roots of his bones.

He had a great fear of heights. Something to do with when he was a lad and fell from a local church roof if he believed what his friend, Sigmund Freud had told him. *But you never know with those brain shrinks,* he thought with a grin on his face. Often they're as nuts as the people they help.

Then he caught himself. *Does that make me nuts then?*

Then something odd struck his fancy. Urgently odd. He turned to face Holmes once more. He cleared his throat to gain his attention. Holmes glanced at him.

"One thing, Holmes."

"Yes."

"Since when did you know how to drive?" Watson asked, his eyebrows screwed together in doubt.

Holmes smiled. "I don't."

Watson gave him a look of extreme terror. "We're all going to die!"

Nightmare

Watson shook his head. He let out a sigh of relief. Holmes smiled at him. "You sounded like you didn't like your little dream."

"I had this dream you were driving our car and you don't know how to."

Holmes smiled as he steered their car onto a side road. "Truly remarkable dream, that one."

Watson glared at Holmes, then realized Holmes was steering the car with his knees.

"Holmes! Look out!"

Something huge ran onto the road, blocking their path. Vaguely human, but covered from head to foot in bloody mud. It was both detestable and gruesome at the same time; though Watson couldn't think of why because he was too busy screaming for his life.

Their vehicle struck the humanoid shape and then careened off the road, spinning out of control. But on the windshield, a leering face of utter horror and terror leered through the window at Watson and mouthed one word over and over. He would remember it until the day he died, which looked to be any moment now!

He screamed again as their car spun off the road, then slid sideways across a thick path of dust and small rocks, sending up swarms of rock and dirt into the air behind them.

At that crazy moment, Watson remembered his childhood when his father had tossed him up in the air and how helpless he had felt, but this was pure terror.

The car cart-wheeled head over tail with him and Holmes flying helter-skelter away from it, the earth below rushing up to smack them and the car dropping from above to crush them.

He screamed!

Watson stepped into the sitting room, which Holmes had not left the entire night before. His eyes were as bloodshot as in Watson's nightmare, but his face had the hint of an amused smile on it, as Watson stepped next to him.

"Better now, Watson?"

"Quite, no thanks to you," Watson growled.

"Tea?"

"Very well, if you insist."

"I do."

Watson had pigged out on a whole tray of scones the night before. No wonder he had those nightmares he thought to himself. He would never admit his gluttony had brought him such abject terror, but he was also quite sure by the way that Holmes smirked at him, that the good fellow knew already.

But rather than rubbing it in as he could have, Holmes poured a cup of tea from a nicely decorated china pot into a porcelain cup, placed a spoon next to it, then shoved a small finger bowl of sugar next to that.

Watson sat down with a sigh on his lips, took the

spoon and gave himself three heaping teaspoons full of sugar, stirred several times, then drank.

"Better now?"

Watson gave Holmes a wary look. "Why do you ask?" He looked at the windows. It was early morning and the sun was barely peeking above the neighboring rooftops.

Watson drank another sip, feeling better as the warmth coursed through his throat and into his stomach, leaving it basked with a warm, cozy feeling.

He eyed the tabletop, which except for the teapot, cups, spoons, and sugar was littered with smashed clumps of paper, hastily scribbled, then abandoned; mashed swabs; overturned test tubes; nasty smelling liquids that caused Watson's nostrils to clench tight.

But it was all in a night's work for the two of them and sometimes a night and a day when he was also working alongside Holmes, which he expected was what was coming next.

"All-nighter, hey?" Watson asked before sipping his tea again. No use in objecting to the smell. It was usual with Holmes. He was like a madman once he had the scent of something he wanted or needed to know.

But then as a medical doctor, he was no less a perfectionist. Lives depended on his carefulness and precision. Holmes's work was no less important.

"A new case, Watson."

"It must be a large one judging by the redness of your eyes. And I thought we were taking on the one in the countryside?"

"That's what has kept me up all night. Too many variables remain unknown. Not good to thrust oneself into a case without all the proper research. That's asking for serious difficulties."

Watson snorted. "As if we never have those."

Holmes threw him a quick smile, and then his eyes fixed once more on the item he had been studying. It was a microscope. A new Tes enhanced one. Nikola Tesla claimed you could see the atoms themselves with it. Watson wasn't so sure about that, but it was very good at what it did...examining in great detail various substances, such as poison and bacteria, even though sometimes what they saw was not necessarily so easily interpreted.

It was, after all, yet a budding science, and having the ability to see such minute detail also required retraining the mind and eye to coordinate the new information crowding through the corridors of the brain cells.

"What are you researching?"

"You remember Joe Mortenson, the famous explorer of the moors? He used to work at the London Greens before he moved on to establish a permanent residence at the York Moors. The one our Good Queen Mary of Scots funded some time back."

Watson set his tea cup down, dabbed at his lips with a cloth, and then nodded. "I've taken Ms. Hudson there a few times. Lovely place. All the beautiful greenery. The flowers. The lovely trees. Water. Some of the most interesting birds I've ever seen as well. And huge moths. Swarms of them. Clouds! Almost makes me wish I were a painter."

Holmes cocked an eye on Watson. "Almost?"

Watson laughed. "Sorry, Holmes, but that's a side of me you're not likely to see."

Holmes smiled. "Maybe so. At any rate, Watson, I suspect this case might be of interest to you as well."

"How so?"

"Take a look for yourself."

Watson leaned into the eyepiece of the microscope, ready to be bored, but then his face registered utter and complete surprise. "But this is impossible."

He looked at Holmes for corroboration.

Holmes shook his head. "It's true."

Watson rushed to his room, already taking off his night robes.

"What's the rush?" Holmes inquired with amusement.

"We haven't a moment to lose, have we then?" Watson declared, entering his room. The door slammed shut.

Country Bound

Watson steered their car onto a side road, then stiffened.

"What's wrong, Watson?"

Watson gave Holmes a worried look. "I've done this before, except you were the driver."

"That was a nightmare."

Watson nodded. "Undoubtedly, but you know how Conan doesn't believe in such things. He's always pointing out that our dreams are our subconscious minds revealing hidden truths."

Ms. Hudson giggled from alongside him on the passenger side. "In that case no wonder you have so many nightmares, your head is always filled with so much nonsense."

He growled. "Just because I love scones a bit too much…"

"And get sick," she added.

"And then nightmares," Holmes added.

"I give up!" Watson pulled over to the side of the road.

"Holmes, you drive."

"I don't know how."

Watson glared at him. "Learn!"

He climbed into the back seat as Holmes got out, shut his eyes, and tried to shut out the bright morning sunlight.

Ms. Hudson smiled as Holmes got behind the wheel.

"That's not true is it, Sherlock?"

He grinned at her.

"Oh!" She replied.

Death's Face

"Watson!"

He woke up, still screaming, his body twisted and broken, shattered upon huge rocks. Holmes lay dead next to him, his head pulped, but his eyes. The eyes stared at him…bloodshot and filled with accusations. Why weren't you driving, Watson? This would never have happened.

"Watson! You must wake up!"

"I am awake, Holmes."

Then he felt his shoulders gripped by invisible hands. Holmes's bloody body was holding him in its grip, the pulped head grinning as only Holmes can. "Wake up, Watson, the game's afoot!"

Watson shook his head hard and shut his eyes, but this time when he opened them, he saw himself on his bed, and Holmes was giving him an urgent, but worried look.

"Damnit, Holmes, must you press so hard!"

"Are you sure you want to go with us tomorrow?"

Watson yawned. "Well, I've already died several times in my dreams; what's one more time, hey?"

Holmes gave Watson a warm grip on his shoulders and smiled. "I'll never let that happen."

The York Moors

Ms. Hudson shrugged a shawl closer about her neck and shoulders as she walked quickly beside Watson's side with Holmes on her other. "What do you expect to find?"

Watson cocked an affectionate eye on her. "Oh, I suspect not much."

She gave him one of those you better not lie to my looks.

He smiled and took her hand in his. "Be patient."

She gave him an askew look but said nothing.

She glanced back at their parked car. Watson had fallen asleep several times and awoken to scream. It was beginning to worry her. But then she smiled. Since when has any day with these two ever been normal?

She giggled.

Both Holmes and Watson gave her surprised looks.

"Here we are, safe and sound," she told them as they approached the entrance to York Park.

Captain Robert McNamara, the Park's guardian, and lone guide stood at the gate's booth door and watched as they approached from their rented Tes car. But you might think at first he was merely a replica of a human by the way he stood there. His body was ramrod straight, his eyes straight ahead. He looked like a mannikin in one of the more posh and expensive Surrey stores in London.

But once they parked their vehicle and climbed out, his frozen smile and facial expression warmed into a more human-looking sort, with a friendly smile, but a crisp military manner. He gave them a smart salute, and then he straightened his tie and hat as they neared and gave them his best and most official smile. "Good morning. I suppose you're here for the summit?"

Holmes stopped, who had been quiet to that point, stood behind Watson and Ms. Hudson, his eyes on the Park Ranger.

"A summit?" Watson asked.

"Why, yes." Park Captain Robert McNamara said, a note of puzzlement in his voice.

He looked at Holmes. "You are Sherlock Holmes, are you not?"

Holmes's turn to look surprised. "I am, but how did you know?"

"Oh, that's easy. I read your fat friend's journal every week." He said happily.

Watson bristled. "Who are you calling fat, sir?"

"Dear!" Ms. Hudson warned him.

The Park Captain looked confused for a moment, and then he gave Watson a double take. "Dear me, gracious God, I didn't mean to offend you, sir. You look so much..."

"Thinner in person?" Watson suggested.

The Park Captain started to answer but stopped when Ms. Hudson did a slice across her throat. "Uh....younger."

Watson brightened. "Oh. I do, hey?"

He smiled at Holmes. "I'm beginning to like this man."

Holmes stepped closer to the Park Captain. "You mentioned a summit?"

"Yes. Inspector Bloodstone said you would be arriving soon. And well...here you are."

Holmes glanced at Watson, who shrugged. First, he'd heard of it.

"Where?" Holmes demanded in a noncommittal voice.

The Park Captain opened the gate for them and indicated a path that swept downwards into the major portion of the Moors, where the water and flowering plants were the thickest. "Follow the path."

"Thank you, Captain," Holmes replied.

The Park Captain saluted, and then stepped out of their way. As they passed Watson couldn't help but remark. "Younger, hey?"

Again, Ms. Hudson did a slice of her neck. The Park Captain smiled graciously. "Oh, so much younger, sir."

Watson laughed happily and followed Holmes. Ms. Hudson looked at the Park Captain and gave him a look of relief. He gave her one back, closed the metal gate, and went back inside his tiny booth where he went back on guard once more, standing stiff as a statue, like the guards about Windsor Castle.

Crime Scene

Inspector Bloodstone stood over a human form draped with thick burlap, while his son and several other Constables used a lightweight raft they had constructed from supplies in London. They were poling through the moors water, two poling, while Constable Evans, dressed impeccably as ever, but with splashes of mud on his ankles and boots, poked at the water, made a face, then motioned for his fellow Constables to move on.

"I'm afraid they won't find what they're looking for," Watson told the Inspector as, huffing and puffing, he stopped beside him.

"That so?"

Watson nodded. "Holmes let me look at the sample you sent to him."

"And?"

"I'm afraid that whatever did this to Joseph Mortenson will never be known."

The Inspector turned to Holmes, who was watching Watson closely. "You agree?"

"That was not why I let him look at the sample. I was letting him do so for another reason."

Watson's turn for a surprise. "How so?"

Holmes motioned to the moors. "I was merely looking for some kind of clue to direct our search better."

Watson nodded. "What clued me into his death was the preponderance of uric acid. It is quite heavy once a person has expired. Tends to pollute whatever is about it for several meters at the very least."

Constable Evans shouts, "Found the body!"

Everyone turns about to watch as several of the boats close in on Constable Evans and help him to secure what he has found. It is slowly raised with the help of several long poles with nets.

When it has raised above the water. A man comes into view. The head flops over towards Watson's view.

Society of York Park

The cabin overlooked the park lands and was nestled in a grove of Spruce and Maple trees so it wasn't seen from a distance. No one was hiding there, but it helped to keep interested when certain meetings happened and needed to be discrete as well as unseen by tourists or others.

And so this night was like any other, the visitors quiet and certain as they entered the overly large cabin's front room, where an old-fashioned fireplace spewed smoke into the now dark skies. Anyone looking in that direction now would still not see the cabin, because the smoke was filtered in such a way as to cause it to disperse very quickly once it struck the air.

You see, it wasn't just an ordinary cabin, but one in which seekers of truth gathered and met. The Secret Society of Anthropologists of Greater Britain met there once a year. In secret. Unknown to all, not even their wives and mistresses.

This meeting was more important than most because a great find had been made but at the cost of a living being. Or at the very least the only one they knew of for certain.

The bear of a man who stood next to the fireplace bore a scornful look on his face, as he searched the looks of his comrades gathered before him. "It's not good."

"Aye!" Voices of agreement and approval came from about the room.

Tall men, short men, men of wealth, men of education, and men of royalty sat amongst each other as one. There were no distinctions at the meetings. They all shared the same food. The same drink. The same banter. But tonight was different: They shared fear.

"We must do something." A shorter man with huge walrus mustaches stated but said no more.

Again. "Aye!" Voices of agreement and approval came from about the room.

Sir Frederick Stark, the bearish man, shrugged and turned to look into the fire. He had known the dead man, Joseph Mortenson, for many years. They had braved many an adventure together. It was ironic that this adventure…not one at all…should have created his death.

But the fact remained he had warned Joseph. Warned him to be careful. To stay out of the moors. But more importantly, never to go anywhere alone.

He just hadn't said why.

And Joseph, he should have known, laughed it off, saying, "Why should I and not you?"

Frederick had no reply because to do so would have been to give away a powerful secret. One, he was sworn to keep that way at any cost.

.His voice was so powerful, rich, and full that no man in the cabin could fail to hear even his faintest of whispers. "But what? What must we do?"

The shorter man tweaked his mustaches, and then looked into the glass of common wine that he shared with his brothers of learning. "What can we do? It is done. There is...nothing...nothing at all we can do now."

Frederick turned about to face the shorter man. "There must be a sacrifice."

"Aye." All joined in, but then as they realized what they had agreed to, a dead silence filled the room.

The shorter man stood up. "We're not savages!" He insisted, and then sat back down.

"No. We're not." Frederick agreed. "But sometimes a sacrifice must be made. You know why we are gathered here. Why do we gather here each year? Why we will continue to gather here each and every year until we are no more upon this cursed planet," he hissed. "If not us, then who will protect those who come here? Who?"

"He harmed one of them. We cannot let that pass. It was justice."

Frederick snarled, "It was murder!"

"Was not the other?"

Frederick had no reply to that accusation because it was true. It didn't matter that Joseph had made a mistake like any of them might have; he just had, and that had sealed his doom.

"But he died. Isn't that enough?" The shorter man interrupted.

"No. It's awake now. It thirsts."

The men in the room paled at those words.

He repeated them to further cement his unspoken demand. "It thirsts!"

"Aye." All the men replied as one. But the shorter man had not joined in.

He fidgeted with his cup of wine, his thoughts elsewhere when he felt a grip of iron on his right shoulder. He looked up.

Frederick looked into his eyes. "Sacrifices must be made!"

Bloated Corpse

"It's him." Watson agrees, comparing the body's face to the photograph that Inspector Bloodstone holds for him to look at.

"I agree," Holmes added.

He glances at where the body was found.

"And where was the sample uric acid found, Watson?"

"You know that better than I, you're the one who summoned me to join you," Watson responded irritably.

"Stay with me, Watson. Because this changes everything."

"How so? He did, after all, die here in the moors."

Holmes eyed the water-bloated corpse laying face up at his and Watson's feet. The Inspector and his son were helping pack up things for the return to London behind them.

"The uric acid was not found where Mister Mortinson's body was."

"And?"

Watson got what Holmes was leading him to. "Distance. By Jove, you're right. The Uric acid was not found even close to that spot and it couldn't possibly have emitted from there. Too far away, even with a drift, which I'm sure there is as the moor waters constantly replenish from their underground springs, but even so, they would not have drifted to the spot the chemicals were discovered."

Holmes waited, there was more.

Watson's eyes rounded as he realized where this was all heading.

"By God, Holmes, it wasn't human urine at all!"

"Agreed, Watson," Holmes replied with a pleasing look. "It would take a giant to emit that much urine!

Constable Evans, who had overheard the conversation as he picked up a net, stopped and turned to his friends. "Or something else."

Watson and Holmes turned to look at him.

"What are you suggesting, Constable?" Holmes asked.

"There have been rumors."

"Yes, yes."

"Rumors of a beast."

Holmes bit at his lower lip.

Watson suddenly remembered his nightmare and blanched, but he said nothing.

"What kind of beast?"

"Some kind of moor beast or monster that pulls its victims into the mud and drowns them."

The Inspector joins them.

Holmes nodded. "That may be true. It remains to be seen if it is, in light of no evidence to such, but there is also a distinct and remaining possibility."

"Which is?"

"That more than one person died out there."

The Inspector explodes. "Do you know what that means, Holmes?"

"Yes, we could have a serial killer loose."

Watson shuddered. "I much prefer that to the alternative."

"Which is, Watson?" Holmes asked, his face showing he might be onto something.

Watson smiled. "More than one murderer."

Holmes nodded. "In that, you could be right."

The Inspector turned sharply upon Holmes. "A double murder then. By two different killers?"

On Holmes's look, he said, "Four times?"

Holmes remained silent.

"My God, Holmes, what are we dealing with here? Another cult?"

"That remains to be seen," Holmes commented, his face unreadable.

"Rubbish and nonsense, my good fellow," Watson told Holmes. "One man could not exude that much uric acid. Not even a dozen! And the likely hood of even a cult urinating in the same spot. Zero!"

Holmes gave the Inspector and Watson one of his more grim smiles. "Who said it was a man?"

Deadly Silence

Outside the cabin, the sleeping animals in the woods and the fowl of the sky all were startled awake by the outcry of a dying man. They stirred, not sure if they should flee if they were safe or not, but the sound had stopped; it came no more.

Silence fell once more upon the park.

And upon another.

The Path for Clues

Holmes and Watson stood on the edge of the moors, taking a breather. They had been scouring the perimeter of the moors for hours now. Holmes took his deerstalker cap and swiped his face to get at the sweat that was threatening to drizzle down his scalp into his face.

Dry again, he replaced the cap and then eyed the distance they had traveled and what yet remained.

Watson gave him a worried look. "Do you think Ms. Hudson will be all right by herself?"

Holmes smiled. "She's with Constable Evans and the Inspector. How could she be any safer?"

Watson nodded. "I suppose. But I would have felt better had she stayed with us."

Holmes put a hand on Watson's right arm and squeezed gently. "Dear John, sometimes we have to let go of those we love to draw them closer."

Watson looked into Holmes's eyes a moment and looked away. "Still."

Holmes laughed and hiked the backpack he was carrying over his left shoulder to his right. "Come, we still have much more ground to cover before it gets dark."

Watson looked at him. "You mean we're staying here overnight?"

Holmes smiled. He didn't answer. He just kept walking; his eyes watching the perimeter of the moors waters for tell-tale signs. Signs of egress.

Watson marched alongside him, still worried, but resigned. "I wish I had a scone. At least that would soften the blow of this miserable hike."

"Here!" Holmes said.

Watson looked over and Holmes held out a scone.

Watson gave him a surprised look and took it. He held it as if it were precious gold.

"How?"

"Mrs Hudson told me to do this if you got unruly or out of control," Holmes replied with a laugh.

Watson almost dropped the scone. "If I what!"

"Holmes!" He cried out as Holmes kept on walking, ignoring him.

Watson shrugged his shoulders finally and worked to catch up, but not so fast as to lose the scone, which he hurriedly began making short work of.

Beast

Ms. Hudson sighed and sat down on a rotting log to take her shoes off. She emptied them, allowing small rocks and pieces of rotting wood to fly away. "This place is a good substitute for a first-class garbage dump," she said with a sigh that sounded very suspiciously like a growl that Watson made.

Inspector Bloodstone and Constable Evans both almost broke into laughter. She sounded so much like Watson at that moment.

She looked up. Startled. "Oh my! I'm becoming John!" She admitted.

Then they laughed.

Something large splashed in the reeds about five yards offshore.

The Inspector reached into his jacket for his weapon. As did Constable Evans.

They all tensed, waiting to see what would happen next.

Silence.

More silence.

Nothing.

The two men relaxed and began to put their weapons away.

"I thought the moors were safe," Ms. Hudson told them.

Inspector Bloodstone gave her a neutral look. "It should be."

Then something rose in front of them, water streaming from its body as it grew taller and taller before them until it towered almost five feet above them. It was huge. Larger than any animal either man had seen before and it stood on two legs. Its entire body was covered with matted fur that more resembled that of a soggy tree trunk than of true hair. It dripped gobbets of mud and thick moors water.

"Oh dear God!" Ms. Hudson muttered.

The Inspector whipped his gun up.

Ms. Hudson ran forward and stopped him. "Don't!"

He tried to break free as the creature continued to stand there, its bloodshot eyes fixed on him as he struggled with the female, then it descended back into the moors waters and out of view.

"Father!" Constable Evans shouted.

The Inspector suddenly realized whom he had been struggling with.

"Dear God, Ms. Hudson, don't ever do that again!"

"You mustn't shoot something just because it frightens you," she scolded him.

"I will damn well shoot it, especially if it's huge like that monster was and glares at me like I'm ham over a fire!"

When Ms. Hudson just glared at him, the Inspector looked away and shook his head. His gun hand was shaking. "I'm getting too old for this nonsense."

"Well, Inspector," Ms. Hudson told him brightly. "I pretty much doubt anyone is old enough for that thing we just witnessed."

The Inspector gave her a close look. "You recognized it; didn't you?"

"Yes," she told him. She looked at him first, then the Constable. "I didn't want to say anything at first, because I didn't want to frighten you, poor fellows."

Constable Evans broke into laughter. His father looked at him and he immediately shut up until his father looked away and then he muffled his laughter with one hand over his mouth and pretended to be doing something else, by kicking at the reeds nearest the shore.

"Well, I dare say, Ms. Hudson, I can't be any more

frightened of that creature had you told me earlier we might be meeting up with him. It was him, wasn't it?"

She blushed.

"Oh!" He gasped. "I beg your pardon."

"Accepted."

She turned to Constable Evans. "I don't think this is what took the life of Joseph Martin. They are too docile."

"How do you know this?" He asked.

"Because...don't tell John this, he thinks all I do is cook and clean, but I have a life beyond the kitchen and living rooms..." She admitted with a touch of pride. "I am a junior anthropologist."

She swelled with pride. "I just finished earning my Junior Woman Pride of Paleoanthropologist badge this last week."

"A what?" The Inspector asked, a bit dismayed at her account.

"I study life that no longer exists."

"Well, Ms. Hudson that which we just witnessed is not living in the past," the Inspector pointed out.

"And that means then that there are men who might use such a creature to their ends," she threw back at him.

"Why would you say such a thing?" he demanded.

"How could any man tame such a beast?"

"That's assuming it's a beast," Ms. Hudson told him, her eyes narrowed with anger still.

"I'm sorry, I just can't believe something like that would need to be told to murder someone…for any reason whatsoever!"

"Who said anything about the reason?" Ms. Hudson demanded. "Murder is not the weight of reason acting intelligently, but of power and control coming in to dominate one's better senses and still the soul and heart to a cold, despicable deed."

The Inspector backed up as if swatted, then gave her a new look of appreciation. "I do believe Watson would be most surprised by this Ms. Hudson."

"Most," Constable Evans agreed, a grin on his face, which was not lost by Ms. Hudson, who gave him a warm smile in return.

"Doctor Watson hasn't a clue how much of a woman you are, Ms. Hudson, does he?" Constable Evans asked.

She dimpled sweetly. "I don't want to disillusion him. He's so used to me just being a landlady, that he finds it hard at times to see the real me," she admitted. Then as conspiratorially as before. "So, please do not expose my interest to him. I wouldn't want to make him feel challenged in any way by being with me," she insisted.

Constable Evans crossed his heart.

The Inspector nodded. "In my mind, he needs such challenges; he is a bit too testy to my taste at times with you and us."

"Were you to rest as little as that man, you would be…" she grinned. "…Testy as well."

The Inspector nodded. He wasn't about to argue with this woman, especially on a point that his son, Constable Evans, reminded him of frequently.

He looked at the moors. "It's getting dark. We need to be heading back. We won't get anything more done now. We'll return tomorrow with more men and do a thorough search."

"I agree," Ms. Hudson said. "But rather than return to London, wouldn't it be better to stay here?"

"How?"

"I know a cabin we can meet at and stay until the morning. So we need not return yet. It's quite dangerous at night sometimes when the Vipers come out from their places of warmth seeking food for the evening.

"Nonsense." The Inspector insisted. "We're perfectly safe..."

He froze midsentence. Something brushed his right leg. He looked down as a viper raised its head to look at his leg and then it lowered its head, slithered over his shoe, and into the waters.

He gulped.

"On second thought!"

A Cry in the Dark

"We best seek shelter, Watson," Holmes insisted. "I don't think we can make it back in the dark."

"I agree," Watson said. "The dratted sun fell much faster than I thought it would."

"It's winter. The clouds have covered it prematurely," Holmes pointed out.

"Everything's premature in our line of work," Watson commented. "Where then?"

"Ms. Hudson mentioned there was some kind of retreat to our left some way back. It will only be another half hour or more before we can reach it. She told me it is stocked with provisions and firewood, as well as several beds."

"But what of her and the others?"

Holmes smiled. "I suspect they are already there and waiting with a toasty fire for us."

Watson's stomach growled loudly. "I wish it were stocked with toasty scones as well."

Holmes grinned, and then slapped his backpack in a friendly fashion.

Watson's eyes rounded. "Oh God bless you, Ms.

Hudson!"

"Indeed, Watson. Indeed!"

"And God bless you, Holmes, for hiding them from me."

"I made sure to saturate the backpack with tobacco stains on the inside."

Watson brightened. "You tricked me!"

"And quite successfully," Holmes replied, pleased with how Watson was responding. He nodded and cut in front of Watson, heading for a side path they had passed but minutes before.

Watson followed after Holmes as he headed for the cabin.

Watson smiled. "God, how I love that woman!"

As they walked Holmes noted something on the ground near the water. He paused a moment to look more closely. Watson stopped too and looked. "Something large fell here? And look, Holmes, another nearby!"

"Put your foot in the imprint, Watson."

"But why..."

"Humor me, my friend."

Watson sighed and put his already wet left shoe into the print. It descended into the mud and murky water and debris flooded over the top of his shoe. He started to jerk it back. Holmes stopped him.

"Wait!"

"A vial please, Watson."

Watson automatically reached into the black bag that never left him and plucked a vial out. Holmes took it, stooped into the water slowly so as not to disturb it further, and swabbed the debris about Watson's foot. He put the swab into the vial and handed it to Watson, who placed it into his bag.

"Have you no idea yet what your foot is standing in?" Holmes asked politely.

Watson stared at his foot, and then as he looked a bit closer, he saw that his foot was enclosed by a rough shape approximating another foot.

He looked up at Holmes, who grinned.

"Judging by the size of your foot inside the other, I'd say our friend stands at least nine feet tall, perhaps a foot more or less," Holmes added.

"That's very large for an animal or human."

"In America, there is a creature known as the Grizzly Bear. It can walk on its two hind legs and stands up to ten feet tall when stretched," Holmes informed Watson.

"Yes. But this isn't America."

"True. This means that whatever we have found the footprint of, is most certainly not any animal we have ever known."

A sudden horrible sound echoed across the moors.

Both men turned to look.

Nothing.

Nothing moved.

No movement.

"That sounded like a man's cry." Watson declared.

"A very large one," Holmes said.

Watson shook his head. "God knows what kind of beast wears that foot."

"As long as it doesn't wear us, dear Watson, then I am fine with it." Holmes jested. Then he plucked several long hairs from a reed he had spotted and placed them in a new vial which he motioned Watson to hand over, then got to his feet and continued the hike to the cabin.

Watson followed, but his eyes kept drifting back to the footprint. "A creature with a foot that large would have to be a giant."

Holmes said nothing. His face was tight with strain. He didn't dare yet put a voice to his suspicions.

A second cry sound in the moors. Much louder.

Human! And terrified!

Then a second cry, this time louder still, and filled with despair and hopelessness.

Holmes and Watson glanced at each other, then ran towards the source of the sound.

Bloody Hell

"What's that smell?" The Inspector asked, sniffing as he entered the cabin after Ms. Hudson, who began flinging window curtains aside and raising windows to let fresh air inside.

"God awful is what it is!" Ms. Hudson complained as she continued opening windows. "Those men never clean properly."

"But odd…" She said, and then paused.

"Odd what?"

She pointed to the floor near the fireplace and the fireplace. "Someone's been here before us. And not that long ago."

"How can you tell?"

She bent down and rubbed her finger across the floor, then raised it before his eyes. "No dust."

Constable Evans said nothing. His eyes were on the center of the large room, where a bright red stain reflected moonlight from its surface.

"Bloody hell!" Constable Evans gasped.

Inspector Bloodstone and Ms. Hudson spun about to see what was disturbing him. Then they saw what he was looking at.

Before either could react, a horrible cry of utter pain and loss burst through the open windows.

Giant of the Moors

Holmes and Watson ran as fast as they could along the shore of the moors until they reached an opening that delivered a large quay into the moors and some posts for tying off small boats.

They stopped.

In the center of the moors were now visible about ten boats. Something large stood amid the circle of boats and was lowering into the water, holding something in its arms.

The boats began to turn around and head back to where they stood.

"Holmes."

"I think it best we retreat from here, Watson. And pray they are not looking our way."

Watson nodded.

They turned about and spotted a path, heading up into a large grove of trees.

"This must be where the cabin is hidden." Holmes pointed out as they climbed the steep, but a smooth path.

Something slithered out of Watson's way and he let

out a tiny shriek.

Holmes looked back.

Watson had his weapon out and aimed at a snake slithering into the smaller brush. "Watson."

"I hate the damn things!" Watson cursed.

"Not now!"

Watson lowered his pistol, and then looked at Holmes. "Sorry. It's just..."

"We'll talk about it later." Holmes insisted and continued upwards.

They were halfway up the incline when they were met by Ms. Hudson, Constable Evans, and the Inspector.

"Inspector," Holmes greeted. "Ms. Hudson. Constable Evans."

Ms. Hudson flung herself into Watson's eager arms. She began to cry softly.

Holmes looked from her to the Inspector, who shook his head and then gestured towards the moors. "I suspect you already know the source of her grief."

Holmes and the others turned to look as the men on the boats landed on the quay and began disembarking.

"Perhaps," Holmes said.

Then he turned to Constable Evans. Holmes's eyes were blazing with a familiar light always there when he was excited.

"How fast can you reach the vehicles? I'm going to need something."

Holmes demanded.

He looked back to the approaching boats. "And fast!"

Secret Society

The Secret Society of Anthropologists of Greater Britain entered the cabin, one by one, expecting nothing to change.

Frederick was the first to notice the blanket over the middle of the floor.

"Someone has been here," he warned.

"The windows have been opened," a fat man noted, as a sharp breeze came through from behind him, catching his attention.

"All of them!" Another spoke up.

Frederick stiffened.

He put a finger to his lips, then reached into his heavy overcoat and brought out a weapon. The others froze. Was he going to shoot one of them?

"That won't be necessary," Holmes told the man as he strode into the room from the only other room in the large structure. He was smiling and had his hands out to show they were empty.

"Who are you?" Frederick demanded, finger tightening on the trigger of his weapon.

"Holmes, Sherlock Holmes!"

Every man in the room gasped. They backed up as if an army stood before them, but Frederick was unimpressed.

"You seem quite calm for a man who faces a dozen and a gun aimed at your heart. And…" he grinned. "…I never miss!"

"I suppose you don't, old man," Holmes replied, flinging a small vial he had held in his right hand.

It flew through the air and smashed into Frederick, who gasped at first, but when he saw a yellowish stain spreading down his jacket, he laughed.

"Nice try, Holmes, but I am not frightened of a bit of urine."

The other men broke into laughter and came closer, their faces grim and threatening as they looked at Holmes.

Holmes beamed at them. "I have to admit the lot of you caught me somewhat by surprise. But fortunately, my good friend, Watson, secured a sample which you have so handily allowed me to display for you…upon your jacket."

"That'll cost you, Mister Holmes," Frederick shot back with a snarl.

"Undoubtedly it will not cost me, but you sir."

Frederick gave Holmes a blank look.

Watson came out beside Ms. Hudson, who looked tense, but tried to put on a brave smile, though distressed in doing so.

One of the men gasped. "I know you! You're Ms. Hudson...the..."

Ms. Hudson gave him a look that could kill and he hurriedly backed away and shut up.

Frederick eyed the man speculatively and then turned back towards Holmes once more. He didn't put his weapon away.

"I believe you are lying, Mister Holmes."

Holmes's smile vanished. It was replaced with a grim visage. "Since when has murder become acceptable behavior for your society?"

The men about them gasped in alarm, and began panicking, wavering in fright.

"Quiet!" Frederick shouted. "He can't prove a thing. And if I shot the lot of them; the police would say nothing. They're trespassing!"

Everyone shut up.

Ms. Hudson looked about, recognizing many of the men. She appeared ready to burst into tears again as she did so. Watson put an arm about her shoulder and squeezed gently. She sagged against him, soaking up his warmth and protectiveness. She didn't know what to make of what these men had become. *What had been done here!*

Frederick motioned to Holmes. "And does the Great Detective have any clues as to why I know who you are?"

"Because a man of your reputation reads the paper as do all men of your merit and my good friend and partner, John Watson here has ably chronicled my adventures within their pages."

Frederick nodded.

He looked at the others. "I'm sorry."

The meaning behind his words became evident as he tightened his grip on the trigger of his weapon and turned to aim it at Holmes once more. "But this meeting needs to be adjourned for another year, and this is as good a time as any to do so."

Watson spoke up. "I wouldn't do that, if I were you, sir!"

Frederick gave Watson an appraising look as he looked at the weapon in Watson's hand. "Perhaps I've underestimated you, people."

He gave them a smile that radiated pure malice.

"Perhaps not!"

He nodded his head.

A group of men rushed from the back room and grasped Watson and Holmes by their arms. Several from the interior of the room grabbed Ms. Hudson.

"How dare you touch me?" She gasped.

Watson's face turned beet red. "You harm one hair on her..."

Frederick moved so quickly that Watson had no chance to react. The pistol in Frederick's hand slapped Watson across the side of his head and he collapsed to the floor, the men holding him unable to sustain his dead weight.

"No!" Cried out, Ms. Hudson. She tried to go to Watson, but the men restrained her. She stomped on the foot of one and got several feet, before two more grabbed her and slammed her against the wall, pinning her arms behind her back.

"You'll regret that," Holmes warned.

Frederick turned to Holmes. "And tell me how, Mister Great Detective. Tell me how that shall come to pass?"

Holmes's face turned stone cold. His smile vanished and he said with such menace in his voice that every man in the room shivered with fear for a moment.

"You shall die, of course!"

Frederick broke into laughter. "No, Mister Holmes, you will!"

He aimed his weapon to fire.

Change of Plans

A roar of great outrage came from outside.

Frederick pivoted to cover the door. There was only one thing, one creature that could make that sound.

The men in the room all cowered back, looking for a way out. Some ran into the back room and vanished.

Frederick waited, his weapon trained on the entrance.

Nothing.

No more sounds.

Satisfied, he turned back to face Holmes, who hadn't moved one bit.

Frederick looked unsettled for a moment and then smiled. "Even the Great Detective knows better than to run outside right now."

"What have I to fear of the outside, Sir?" Holmes demanded, the twist of a smile upon his lips.

"Everything, Mister Holmes. Everything!"

"I agree. You should," Holmes said quietly, his body tensing. "But I, for one, shall not be there to greet death when he arrives for you."

"Then whose, if not yours!" Frederick demanded,

raising his pistol to fire into Holmes's chest. Holmes's look was finally shaking his nerves up.

Ms. Hudson looked up from beside Watson, whose head was in her lap, and cried out. "Don't!"

"What do I care about your words?" Frederick demanded.

"Not you!" She cried out and pointed.

Frederick turned about to look, but too slowly. Something huge stepped into the room so fast that he didn't have a chance.

It grabbed him from behind and then lifted him high in the air. His weapon fell to the floor.

Frederick screamed. "Someone help me!"

One of the men near the door tried to flee behind the creature and it smashed Frederick into the fellow, sending him flying to the ground outside.

"Help me!" Pleaded Frederick again as the creature looked into his eyes.

The creature gave the barest hint of a smile. "Sometimes a small sacrifice must be made," it uttered in horrible broken English.

The creature of the moors took Frederick and snapped his spine as easily as we might snap a piece of twig. It puffed its chest angrily and then dropped

Frederick to the floor. It stomped into the room towards Holmes, who didn't budge.

Ms. Hudson stood up and faced the creature. "You will not harm anyone else in this room! Do you hear?"

The creature gave her a curious look and stepped closer. She stepped in front of the men and shook a fist at the creature. "I will not let you harm either of them!"

The creature gave her an odd look and cocked its head as if trying to understand her words.

"Hurt?" it said with a mushy voice.

"Hurt!" She shot back, not budging. "These men are your friends. They would never harm you!"

The beast eyed Holmes and the fallen Watson, then her again. "Ma...ma...mother?"

Ms. Hudson smiled.

The beast nodded, then turned, ducked low, and exited the cabin, leaving behind smashed panels of wooden floor and the body of the dead Frederick.

Ms. Hudson began to tumble to the ground.

Holmes caught her into his arms.

"Well done, Ms. Hudson. That was the best bluff I have ever witnessed."

"It wasn't a bluff, you silly man!"

Holmes sat her down on one of the chairs of the

room, and then kneeled next to Watson. He gently tapped his face, and then massaged his neck muscles for several long moments. His face was filled with worry until Watson's stomach growled almost as loud as the beast that had just come inside and exited.

Watson's eyes opened. He looked into Holmes's face. "Is it time for dinner yet?"

Ms. Hudson burst into laughter.

Holmes smiled.

He gave Watson a gentle squeeze of his right shoulder. "Always Watson. Always."

Seeking to Escape

The men of The Secret Society of Anthropologists of Greater Britain flooded along the path towards their vehicles, some faster, some slower, but all determined to reach their card and depart the area, never to return.

As their vehicles came into view they cried out happily. The nightmare was almost over. The leading two dashed faster only to cry out, then five more were caught as a series of nets fell from above. They had been hanging in the tree foliage and triggered to fall by their passing over the ground beneath.

Constable Evans and his father stepped into view, weapons leveled as the men struggled to break free. The men froze and stopped struggling to break free.

"Right smart of you boys," the Inspector told them.

"The other men got away, father!" Constable Evans warned.

The Inspector gave his son a grim smile, and held up a piece of paper." A little something the gate guard gave me when we entered earlier. Every one of these men's names is on it. Every single one," he said with a grin.

Ms. Hudson on the Attack

Ms. Hudson sat near Watson, holding his hand as he scooped up a scone to devour it. It was late. Very. Very late, but she didn't care. Watson had a terrible lump on the side of his skull from the pistol-whipping.

"I'm all right. I've had worse," Watson told her when she wouldn't stop staring at the wound.

"You're a doctor, how would you know?" She asked him and then giggled.

He smiled. "I love you."

"And I love you as well, you hard-headed old tortoise, you!"

He gave her a stern, reprimanding look. "Who are you calling old?"

They both laughed. But only for a few moments, before he reached for his fourth scone of the night.

"I only regret one thing," she told Watson.

"What, my dear?"

"That more men like them will replace their positions."

He smiled at her. "How likely is that to happen?"

"Very," she snorted angrily. "They always buy the

positions, leaving us poor women out of the loop!"

He gave her a surprised look.

"The government needs to have fairly elected officials, not those nominated by graft and power."

Watson nodded, still puzzled by her words, and then said, "They should have known better than to sanction murder. I hope they all rot in hell!"

Her angry frown vanished as he took her hands between his and squeezed them lovingly. "I wish it were not the world we live in sometimes, but the reality is sometimes slow to catch up to our dreams. Someday, even a woman like you will lead, even as our Good Queen Mary of Scots."

"But they will go free. They were murderers. All of them!" She insisted. "Even if they didn't do it directly, but instead some poor creature."

"Oh, they will, Ms. Hudson. They will." Holmes assured her as he came into the sitting room with his night robes on. He sat next to the fire, threw on his lap blanket, and held his hands before the warmth.

"Her Majesty, Good Queen Mary of Scots has a special place for them. In her deepest of dungeons. She is a fair person, but none shall escape justice. And I ask you, if that is not hell, it is certainly the closest I would ever want to be. Not one will escape what they have done. She will see to that."

Holmes sighed. "The man they murdered was a man the Queen honored above many. She will not forgive them any time soon."

Ms. Hudson nodded. But she could see there was more. She bit her lower lip but didn't say what it was.

"I know something's bothering you, my dear. Speak up," Watson insisted.

Ms. Hudson looked at him again. "That poor man, Joseph. Why did they murder him?"

"Oh, they didn't murder him, Ms. Hudson," Holmes said as he gazed into the fireplace. "He just happened to step into the wrong place at the wrong time."

He turned from his examination to finish. "The moors have sinkholes in them and unfortunately for him, he found one. One that Frederick had been secretly hiding in, after luring the poor man from his safe path through the moors."

Ms. Hudson cringed. "Then why did those awful men murder one of their companions?"

"Oh, that's simple enough," Holmes told her. "Frederick was in a hideous debt to the murdered man and he had so controlled the others into believing his every word...."

"A cult then?" Watson asked.

"Yes. A cult. And a very dark one." Holmes replied. "He had prepared them for the murder by telling them that the creature would not rest in peace unless one of them died."

"I and the Inspector examined his bank records upon my suspicions and I can only conclude that he has murdered many others based on what we found."

"That's horrible!" Ms. Hudson said, shaking her head.

"And evidently, he used some kind of tale about the monster needing a sacrifice each year or sooner...if the men he killed demanded their money from him."

"Quite despicable, I must say," Holmes said, shutting his eyes.

"That's horrible." Ms. Hudson said, her face pale. "They all had such good names and to let the greed of one man drive them into such a hideous act is unspeakably wrong."

Watson sighed. His old war wound began to ache. "Just like war then. Man against man, brother against brother..."

"Yes, Watson. Just like war. And always for the same pathetic reasons. Power and control. Fortune. In this case, knowledge of the Beast of the Moors would make them all famous and wealthy if they could discover the beast. This is why they made the sacrifice. In hopes of luring it from its hiding place. It had failed all other times but this once."

"But instead it discovered them, did it not, Holmes?"

"Yes," Holmes said with finality. "It did. Finally."

Holmes gave them both a warm glance of amusement, then threw off his lap blanket, and went to the sitting room table where his microscope was set up.

He began examining the sample he had found in the moors.

"Holmes, why did you throw that vial at Frederick?"

Holmes smiled. "You tell me, Watson. You first discovered what was in it."

Watson brightened. "Of course. Animals respond to certain smells. It thought it was about to be attacked."

Holmes nodded. "Yes. You see, that poor fellow who drowned accidentally struck the creature with his pole as he was attempting to escape drowning. He was so frantic that he emitted a large amount of fear...pheromones."

"You mean that beast killed Frederick because he thought he was being attacked?"

"Exactly," Holmes replied.

"And here I thought it was just that no normal male would ever go against my love," he said added, tongue in cheek. "They're no match for her."

Ms. Watson pinched him lightly on the cheek and he let out a mock cry of pain. They kissed.

Holmes looked up. "Oh, but Watson, it was not because it was a male that it backed off."

Watson sighed and put down the fifth scone he was about to pounce upon. "I suppose my beastly stomach is appeased enough for a time." He got up to take a look at the microscope's lens.

"Ah."

He stood up and eyed Ms. Hudson. "It would appear our beast was not man enough to stand up to you."

She laughed and then saw the look on his face. "He wasn't a man?"

Watson shook his head. "This sample clearly shows that the Beast of the Moors was not male, but female."

"A very pregnant one," Holmes said as he stood up, stretched, and reached for his pipe. He stoked it and then lit it up. He went to the window and looked out at the dark skies, but his vision was of the moors instead.

"Does this mean there will be more of those creatures?" Ms. Hudson asked a bit nervously.

"As soon as we returned from our journey I went to the British Museum. A friend of mine there, Doctor Hopkins, allowed me a small tour of prehistoric history."

Watson turned to look at his friend. "A tour? I thought you were seeking evidence?"

"Oh, I was, Watson. I was."

Holmes turned to look at his friends. "You see our scientists for a long time have believed there were giants in the past but had no living proof of such, nor any remains that could be determined to be from such a primate."

"Then what did you find?"

"Not I. Frederick."

Ms. Hudson recoiled with distaste. "I never want to hear that name again. He was a disgusting man with no right to the credentials he wore so proudly."

"Oh, but you are wrong, dear Ms. Hudson," Holmes stated matter-of-factly.

Before Watson could rise to her defense, Holmes went on. "You see, he discovered the beast it seems some ten years ago. It had been in hibernation."

"Primates don't hibernate. Least not human ones." Watson pointed out

"Oh no, John, there is one," Ms. Hudson interjected.

He gave her a look of surprise.

"Fat-tailed dwarf lemurs can hibernate up to 8 months," she informed him.

Holmes stole Watson's reply from him before he could get into trouble. "So you see, Watson, if one could, so could others. Especially ones that are related to the lemur family."

"Are you saying that that giant was a lemur?" Watson stammered. "It certainly isn't the least bit cuddly looking. And it spoke. It can speak rationally."

"I think it more likely it was just mouthing back like a parrot does what it had already heard."

Holmes smiled.

Then mysteriously. "But I could be wrong, of course, I'm not quite as developed in my understanding as Ms. Hudson, I fear.'

Watson cleared his throat and reached for the scone to eat. "I surrender. You always have all the answers, Holmes." But then he remembered something Ms. Hudson said. And Holmes had just said it as well. He turned to give her a stern look.

She shriveled beneath his gaze. But before she could burst into tears, he broke into laughter. "Just how long did you think you could keep hiding the fact that you're a Junior Woman of the Anthropology Society you've been sneaking off to meetings with these last six months or so?"

She gave him a look of utter astonishment. "You've known the whole time and never told me," she snapped furiously.

"Indeed."

Then she blushed with shame at her response. "You aren't angry with me?"

Watson snatched his fifth scone up and gave her a look of utter love and trust. "My dear, a woman who loves me so much that she stays up late at night to feed my savage beast is not a woman I could ever, ever criticize or deny what she loves the most in her heart of hearts."

"Oh, John!" She cried out and flung her arms around him.

Holmes smiled and then headed for his room.

He stopped to look back. "Oh and one more thing."

Watson and Ms. Hudson broke their clench to look his way.

"We must tell Inspector Bloodstone to have a talk with the Park Captain Robert McNamara about the new family he should be expecting soon. I suspect the new family is going to become quite visible in the moors now. Quite so indeed," Holmes said with a light smile, and then exited into his room.

Ms. Hudson gave Watson a smile of utter delight. "Wouldn't it be nice to see her babies?"

Watson shook his head. "In God's name woman, can you imagine the size of the diapers she's going to need?"

They both broke into laughter.

Tracks of death

Its tracks were as plain to see as if one had held a lantern up to a wall streaked with mud all over it. He could smell it as well. It stank of death and dying. Of fear and horror. Of an ending to what might have been longer, but now would never be.

He touched very carefully the beginning of a spot on the rug, then traced it with his carefully manicured nail until it stopped about eight feet above the floorboards, the beautiful tapestry of the wallpaper, the molded window frame, the silver backed glass, the embroidered flags that countered each side of the window and resting just below the ceiling, where the reddish ooze had begun to drip.

"Here," he told his companion.

The man stood in the shadows of the bedroom, examining the body that they had discovered only minutes ago, purely thanks to the very excellent nostrils of Count Dracula.

Holmes tapped his chin with his right index fingernail over and over as he pondered the juxtaposition of the dead woman and the spots of blood on the pink carpet beside the bed, and the spots on the floor beside the ornately designed window where Count Dracula had seen and smelled the initial impurities of death and blood from outside.

"Perhaps," Holmes said, not so sure himself.

He raised his eyes from the pallid figure on the bed, whose throat had been torn open by brute force, allowing a secondary flow of blood to light up the pure white silk sheets it lay upon. Her eyes stared up at him as if accusing him of not being there sooner as if saying, why had you allowed this? That look, which he had seen so many times before, always haunted him, though he never spoke of it. Perhaps that was why the original allure of the opiates had been so strong in him at one time. Over the years he had diminished that, suppressing that futile urge and replacing it instead with a sharp insight honed by clinical knowledge and experience.

Forensics was still a new science in Queen Mary of Scots Victorian England, but one that was gaining more and more proponents, thanks to his and Watson's work.

He had stood alone for years, but now he had a fine team of friends and companions who contributed to his work, helping him to accelerate the time it took to solve a crime and make a difference that he had made in the past, but now sooner, thus sparing more lives over time.

Count Dracula was a part of that team. Not the one of fiction that a parallel Earth called a bloodthirsty vampire, but one of his, who was calm, elegant, and thoughtful of others...though still bearing a sharp pair of fangs...not with the destructive urges that accompanied that of the legendary vampire of the past.

"I'm afraid we shall have to call off the opera tonight," Holmes said.

Count Dracula sighed. He added nothing to the conversation. What was there to say? He was a patient man when it came to facts, and the facts were obvious. Someone or something with very sharp teeth and an enormous amount of strength had destroyed this person.

He found no attraction to these men who deigned to dress like the opposite sex, and pretend to be women, but he also had no particular distaste for them either. People had choices they had to live or die by. This one had chosen to live under a different sky, and their sky had collapsed and fallen upon them for whatever reason. Perhaps lust, perhaps the thrill of dangerous liaisons, who could tell? Surely not Dame Evans who lay

on her regal throne of a bed, her...or rather his...life stricken
from him in one horrid, vampiric moment.

Ironic, that one seeking sexual freedom, had instead found the freedom of death.

"Watson, come here, we need you!" Holmes remarked loudly.

They both heard a thumping from overhead as if a horrible monster were awoken from its repose and was storming for the exit to attend to the intruders below who had disturbed it. The noise grew louder and louder, and Count Dracula tensed, not sure if he was hearing Watson, or something worse.

Then Watson rushed into the room, but without a sound.

Count Dracula, without speaking a word, flung himself out the right half of the window, which lay open and soared upwards like a swift, dark arrow.

"I say, Holmes, whatever got into him?"

"Anything?" Holmes demanded, not commenting on Watson's remark.

"The body perished here in this room, and I cannot for the world of me decide how the blood could have flowed upwards into the room above. It's just an attic, devoid of windows, chimney, or any exit but that which I entered and left but moments ago."

"I see."

Holmes went to the open portion of the double glassed window and gazed at the lawn below. They were two stories up. The attic on the third. He turned slightly to peer at the gabled roof. Searching for the minutest traces of clues that could be there, but found nothing.

"It would seem our murderer either had wings or another method of entering and exiting this home." Holmes decided.

Watson gently shut the eyes of Dame Evans, shuddering, not because of what she was, but what she might have been... a soul with great potential. Dame Evans had been on the brink of a great discovery, one that could have revolutionized the tech industry that had been blossoming under Tesla and Edison.

"Shame."

"Always," Holmes joined with Watson's sympathy.

He steepled his fingers beneath his chin for a moment, nodded his head as if agreeing with someone, and then headed for the exit. "We must let the Inspector attend to this now; we have done all we can. Contact him, will you, Watson?"

"He's going to be disappointed we waited so long to do so," Watson replied."

Holmes gave Watson an amused smile. "Usually, it is he who wakes us. Turnabout is only fair, wouldn't you say, Watson?"

Watson grinned.

He and the Inspector had bones to pick and this time Watson would be justified in picking a very big one.

Watson exited with a happy hum in his throat.

Inspector bloodstone

Inspector Bloodstone exited the Constabulary Wagon alongside Constable Evans, cursing lightly and rubbing his bloodshot eyes until he spotted Holmes and Watson waiting for him at the doorway of the three-story mansion that had once been the home of Dame Evans.

Watson had not waited for him, which made him even more grouchy than usual, because he had then to use his vehicle, which he hated to get dirty. The fog was thick and very heavy with moisture. His new detail work on the car would all be dirty tomorrow morning.

He sighed, he wasn't a martyr, but he felt like one at that particular moment. He got out, letting his son park the car further away in a legal parking spot.

Several older men of a colorful nature stood around Holmes and Watson, chattering obsessively, wiping at their eyes.

"Oh great!" He muttered, cursing the hour and the time of this death.

"What's wrong, father?" Constable Evans asked when he rejoined him.

"Those!" He pointed to the men on the porch. "They look like circus freaks."

Constable Evans sighed.

"What?" The Inspector demanded.

"They are middlings."

"What, for God's sake, are middlings?"

"Men who are neither male nor female. They wear whichever sex they feel like at any particular time."

The Inspector wrinkles his nose in disgust. "I knew there was something off about them."

"Father, you must be more tolerant," Constable Evans chided him.

"I am very tolerant, just not when I'm losing sleep!" He turned to look into his son's face. "Why is it that you never complain?"

Constable Evans smiled. "I learned some years back, before we reunited, to calm myself when such happened and not resent it."

"And?"

"I never found myself tired when I did that."

"Hogwash!" The Inspector growled. "That's just gibberish!" He didn't wait for his son to rebuff his words, but instead launched into, "Why is it always at night this happens, Constable Evans?"

Constable Evans gave his father an amused look. He said nothing. He knew better. When his father insisted on calling him constable, it meant he was in his official grouch mode, and nothing could make a dent in his temperament at such times.

So he said nothing. Instead, he yawned, rubbed the sleep from his eyes, which had closed even less than his father's, and smiled.

Tomorrow would test them both. But tomorrow was tomorrow. Almost as if reading his mind, Holmes looked over and locked onto his eyes for a moment, his hawk-like stare unnerving to most, but to Constable Evans only a sign of the certainty of the man's giant intellect and powers of concentration.

"Where?" Inspector Bloodstone demanded of Holmes as he and his son joined Holmes and Watson.

"Watson, please do the honors."

Watson nodded and headed inside, followed by the Inspector.

Constable Evans gave the three men about Holmes a cursory glance.

The tallest of the three, dressed in all yellow, and with long hair that was braided like a pirate, painted nails and red lipstick, stepped forward and extended his hand. "I am Harold Pinter. A friend of the late Dame Evans."

The second man snickered. "And lover."

"Please!" Holmes scolded the second man. "This is no time for fighting. A man has died here. A man you both claim to be a friend!"

Both men shut up and stood back

Holmes gestured to Constable Evans. "Let's take a walk."

"Where to?"

Holmes didn't answer. Instead, he stepped down from the high porch, which was laden with ornamental flowers and guardian angels, and led Constable Evans about the mansion, his eyes tracing something along their path only he could see. Finally, he stopped.

When he did a dark form descended from above and lit beside them.

Count Dracula eyed the startled Constable, who was reaching for his weapon. "My apologies, Constable, I had forgotten you are a bit nervous about us."

Constable Evans's eyes narrowed. "The woman I loved was drained dry of her life by one such as you," he stated, re-holstering his weapon

"Not one like I, but one whose thirst went above and beyond the mortal boundaries of dignity. I apologize

once more for your loss and offer my condolences."

He gave a regal bow, his eyes filled with a true apology and a touch of sadness. He felt that way because he never drank human blood, nor ever would. But there were rogues in his live stream, who might and did. And they, in revenge for his avoidance of human blood, pretended to be him to sully his name.

Constable Evans looked to Holmes. "So why are we here?"

"Did you notice anything special about any of the men on the porch?"

"Two men of unaccountable taste."

"Or more?"

Constable Evans raised an eyebrow.

Holmes pointed to the roof. "Our friend here, Count Dracula, found a forced entrance upon the roof."

Constable Evans gave Holmes a puzzled look. "But why would they enter that way? Why go to all that effort?"

"Why indeed?" Holmes asked.

He plucked from his cloak something heavy and handed it to the Constable. "When I give the word you are to stab that immediately into the heart of the man I urge you to. You must not hesitate or he will flee."

"Why me?"

"Because the Count would give himself away by his fragrance. When vampires are close to hurting someone, they give off a rare odor that only other vampires can scent. I have another mission."

Holmes gave the constable a stern look. Will you do so, or not?"

"What of Watson?"

"Again. Another mission."

Constable Evans sighed and hefted the small, but still, a quite heavy silver knife.

Count Dracula shuddered at its shape and its deadliness. One of the few things a mortal man could use upon him with success.

"Follow me," Holmes demanded. "Count."

The Count flew upwards, vanishing into the shadows of the roof.

Holmes led Constable Evans to the porch where the two men still stood. He climbed the steps, followed by

Constable Evans, whose right hand was out of sight in the pocket of his trousers.

"I know who murdered Dame Evans."

The two men beside Harold Pinter both headed down the steps, one to the right and one to the left. "We'll

see you later, Harold." One said. "Later!" Said the other.

But as they strode onto the pavement of the sidewalk Watson stepped into view from the right and Inspector Bloodstone from the left.

"What's the meaning of this?" Harold Pinter demanded, his eyes blazing with anger. "Just because we are different is no reason to treat us so inhumanely!"

"Now!" Holmes hammered Constable Evans with his voice.

Constable Evans pulled out his silver knife and plunged it into the heart of Harold Pinter.

The second man tried to rush to his aide but was blocked by Watson and Inspector Bloodstone.

Harold Pinter screamed like a banshee, his voice so horrible that the air was shattered by his terror and anger.

He grabbed for Constable Evans.

Holmes immediately threw a rope of silver about his hands, and then pulled his face down onto the flat of the porch.

Count Dracula descended from above and stood on Harold's back. "Do not move if you value your life, scourge of the night!"

"I shall kill you all!" Harold cried out, frothing blood from his mouth.

From inside the home, a horrible cry broke forth, then a second and a third. A horrible sound like a monster descending from inside erupted, and then Dame Evans stepped forth from inside, his body no longer resembling that of a mortally wounded human, but instead something worse. Something from a nightmare.

"Where is he?" He demanded.

Holmes very calmly blocked the path of Dame Evans.

The monster ground its enormous teeth in his face for a moment, then his horrid shape began to dissolve into that they had seen laying upon the bed. He broke into tears and wept like a woman. Holmes did a very peculiar thing for him and put a hand on her shoulder to comfort him.

Count Dracula

Harold Pinter and the other man were restrained in silver chains. A light smoke rose into the London air as parts of the chains touched the skin of the two men. But neither said a thing, though it was obvious they were in pain.

Holmes and the Inspector watched silently, as the constables then led the prisoners to the back of a Constabulary Wagon. Four constables herded them inside and then climbed in back to watch the prisoners.

The constables made sure both prisoners saw the silver-tipped nightsticks in their hands as they sat opposite them.

"You're going nowhere you like now," one of the constables told the two prisoners. "You even so much as squirm, we'll smoke your rotten brains with our silver. Understand?"

The prisoners didn't reply, but it was obvious they understood because both flinched when the constable waved his nightstick at them.

The back door was shut, and the Constabulary Wagon's huge electric turbine began to spin, sending off a colorful spray of sparks into the air.

Inspector Bloodstone turned to Holmes. "Something has been bothering me, Holmes."

"Yes, Inspector?"

"How did you know it was those two blaggarts and not someone else?"

Holmes smiled. "A little birdie told me."

Watson laughed. "Holmes is teasing you. We discovered that the men had bird droppings on their shoes. The only way they could have gotten that..."

"Was from the rooftop." Count Dracula added with a smirk. "Which is why I flew there."

Holmes nodded. "You see, these men are part of a variety of vampires that can extend their family by ingesting the blood of one such as Dame Evans, a man deluded into thinking he is different from humanity, because of his sexual preferences."

"And he isn't."

"No, Inspector, he is not," Holmes replied, the hint of sadness in his voice. "You see each of us has the same Divine Spark and Dame Evans' only problem is and was his overwhelming desire to belong somewhere he is loved, even if it means dying to our world to join theirs."

Dame Evans stood on the porch watching the door of

the Wagon closed. "But what now? Constable Evans demanded. "He achieved his goal. Now, look at him. More alone than ever before. Now he can never seek human companionship, let alone those vampires we have sent away."

"Yes. But now, he knows them for what they are. For their intent was not to convert him to their cause but to take his life. Had you not stabbed Harold in the heart as you did, the unholy bond they had forged upon him would never have been broken, and he would've awoken..."

"As an Undead Monster." Count Dracula said, shivering with the idea. "Such monsters are the slaves of men like these. Preying upon the innocent. I will not and cannot tolerate vampires of such character."

"But he's still a vampire," protested the Inspector.

"Agreed," Holmes said. "But with a difference. Now he shall be driven by reason like our good Count"

"Thank you, Holmes," the Count said with a grin.

Holmes nodded to him.

"Now, they shall not use his banking knowledge to accumulate ill-gotten wealth for themselves so they can spread further and propagate their cult of evil," Holmes pointed out.

"Who would think vampires could be greedy like mortals," Watson added.

The Count shrugged. "People remain people, even if they crossover to become one of the undead."

"Yes, Watson. Even monsters have, sometimes, peculiar mortal needs," Holmes said with a shrug.

The electric hum of the Constabulary Wagon caught the attention of the three men and they turned to watch as the Wagon drove off.

Behind them, Dame Evans wept softly.

Holmes said, "What strikes me the most about this case, my friends, is that Dame Evans thought he was being born anew, but he was dying to the Light. Better to learn how to love ourselves as God created us than seek to escape in another's flesh. If we do not learn how to love ourselves, others will not either, and then we will be truly alone and an easy target for criminals such as those two now taken away."

Holmes turned to Watson with a smile. "We must rejoice in what we have, not curse that which we do not."

"The only curse I have on my lips right now is that they are not clamping down on a fresh warm scone made by my beloved Ms. Hudson," Watson said, suppressing a yawn as he did so.

Everyone broke into laughter. It had been a long night.

But weren't they all?

Other Books By The Author

Agents of the Crown

Baker Street Universe Tales 1

Baker Street Universe Tales 2

Baker Street Universe Tales 3

Baker Street Universe Tales 4

Baker Street Universe Tales 5

Eighth Voyage of Sinbad

Sherlock Holmes and the Count Dracula Affair

Sherlock Holmes and the Dorian Gray Affair

Sherlock Holmes, Forbidden

Forbidden World

Sherlock Holmes, Frankenstein's Curse

Sherlock Holmes, Gallery of Illusions

Sherlock Holmes, Night Stalkers

Sherlock Holmes, Night Witch

Detective Scotch McBride, That Dark and Dreary Night

Sherlock Holmes, Vampire London

Request for Review

If you found some pleasure in reading my work, please take the time to leave a review for it. Authors can thrive or die for the lack of reviews.

Thanking you in advance for your kindness.

John

Author's Note

I've always had a great love for mystery and adventure. Starting with Agatha Christie's The Bat and ranging to Edgar Rice Burroughs Tarzan of the Apes and Jules Verne's Journey to the Center of the Earth.

It was only a short step between those three writers to run into Sir Arthur Conan Doyle and his wonderful Professor Challenger adventures.

I first read Sir Arthur Conan Doyle's wonderful spread of detective stories when I was still a child. I didn't own books, so I read them at the public library, or at my school library. There was no Internet of Things, no Internet at all at the time. I was very into books as a child, always a loner of sorts. Even though I loved people, I was somehow always more in love with books. Call me bookworm then. Now bookworm writer. Maybe.

I went through the entire adult library in my hometown as a child, reading everything from fiction to non-fiction, science fiction to fantasy, and classic literature to modern. It didn't matter. It was words on paper. I loved the smell of books. Still do, even though I cater to electronic books currently.

This is all a back-story of sorts to give you an idea of why my Sherlock Holmes while based somewhat on the canon of Doyle, are nevertheless much more than that. What would be the point of repeating what's already been done?

No, rather I saw this writing experience as an opportunity to allow my imagination to romp in his playground but take elements from other famous authors and stories I've loved over the years.

Obviously, there are copyright issues when it comes to living authors, so even though I'd love to play in their yards too, that is forbidden territory. So, I have contented myself to take my love of classic literature...Doyle, Verne, Wells, Dumas, Shakespeare and pour them into a mutual melting pot. Kind of a United States of Literature, so to speak.

Whereas the Sherlock Holmes of Sir Arthur Conan Doyle functions out of London, England in the Victorian period; mine exists in a parallel world where all the authors who have ever lived and all their characters are alive at the same time.

Therefore, if you see me including Houdini and Sherlock together, Challenger and Conan Doyle, it makes more sense if they were alive on that world and not this one.

As a person of with a strong scientific background...I wrote a treatise on reaching other dimensions (parallel worlds) as an 8th grader, which my Physics teacher was knocked out about...I believe quite strongly in an unlimited universe, where an infinite number of parallel ones/dimensions exist at the same time.

When I was in India, I found that some there adhere to the belief that everything that man can do or imagine exists in a vast cosmic tapestry so that we do not so much physically exist, as mentally/spiritually move through that infinite tapestry, each choice we make...right or wrong...creating a branching point that we must follow, even though there were already an infinite number of other ones. Awfully close to the parallel world/alternate dimension approach that many scientists are now coming to accept as a reality.

When I was a kid, the scientists barely believed in 4 dimensions...length, breadth, height, and time. Now as an adult there is talk of at least 9 known dimensions.

But getting back to my stories, what makes them relevant and different is that I can populate them with any science, any character, any famous figure, writer, artist or whatever and they all fit! They fit because I created them. For fun. For pleasure. To be able to play on a field of dreams with no end in sight.

So, as you read my stories, dear reader, keep in mind that the Tesla car in my story is not Elon Musk's electric car, but a vehicle invented by collaboration between Thomas Edison and Nicolas Tesla in my invented world. It runs not by electricity as we know it, but by a different energy discovered by Tesla.

In my world Sherlock Holmes is not the first one of the stories, but one of several. Watson, likewise. Just as Spock was duplicated in the Star Trek series of movies to continue their worthy stories, so have I decided to include devices that will stimulate our imagination, take us to places we could never have gone before, and allow me to interject from time to time some of the wonderful insights I have been honored to receive as a maturing adult. So, death exists in my creation, but it has many permutations and outcomes. All exciting and mysterious.

Following this is a description of major characters, as well as items used exclusively in my Baker Street adventures.

Glossary of the Baker Street Universe

A list of players, places and things that take place in the Baker Street Universe created by this author as the playground for his fantasies...and hopefully your own as well.

Bollocks...A common word used by the British to indicate something was nonsense, trash. An expletive.

Drat, dratted...A swear word like damn to indicate frustration.

Tosh...Sheer nonsense and an unkind reference to the upper class at that time.

Tesla Car...Device built by Ford in collaboration with Nicolas Tesla. Powered by a new form of energy unknown to our world yet.

Tesla devices...created by the team of Henry Ford, Thomas Edison, and Nicolas Tesla. Anything from lamps to frigs, to cooking devices. You name it; they've probably invented it in my world.

Moriarity...one of many. Professor Moriarity lives on in many and various manifestations for the sake of conflict, as well as invention and discourse. Where would a great detective be without a great villain to oppose him? While I don't feature Moriarity all the time, be warned he lurks behind the scenes! A lot!

Sherlock Holmes...Young man in his early twenties, comes from a humble home and a good upbringing. Precocious with a perfect memory. Not the cold fish of the Doyle series. Much kinder and humorous. Still with many of the same characteristics, but softened with a gentler personality, without losing the edges that give him an engaging purpose and deductions that are utterly amazing at times.

Watson, Doctor John...hero of the China Wars. Lost first love in China. Now in love with Ms. Hudson. Loves Holmes like a brother. Doctor. Never without his black bag in which he carries his medical supplies and forensics tools that he and Sherlock often use in their investigations. Stocky with a bit of a stomach because of his love of scones, which I constantly use as a play of humor about the man.

Ms. Hudson...not just a landlady anymore, but an integral part of the detective team...supplying support, as well as emotional and sometimes physical support. The glue that binds Watson and Holmes together. Again, in her twenties like Watson and Holmes. Lovely, but not beautiful, except of spirit. Kind and resourceful. Very shrewd and intelligent.

Lady Shareen...Lord Graystone's companion. A beautiful woman with a huge heart. She is responsible for helping women achieve social and financial equality. She also works to uplift the poor and homeless.

Professor Langston...the Invisible Man...a well-meaning doctor, who concocted a cocktail of chemicals that has forever altered his atomic structure such that he can turn invisible at will, though during emotional times of stress he can lose control of his visibility.

Inspector Bloodstone...a cantankerous policeman who has raving red hair, and a temper to match at times. Works with Holmes a lot but prefers to work on his own. Distrusts some of the intuitive moments of Holmes, but overall will go with what he reveals as Holmes is more often right than wrong in his deductions.

Constable Evans...the long-lost son of Inspector Bloodstone. Also red haired, like his father, but with no temper and a great personality. Everyone likes him.

Queen Mary of Scots...has never existed. Instead, this one is a derivation of Mary, who was beheaded and

Victoria. Much more intelligent, progressive, but a leader in every sense of the word.

Magic...exists in this world of Sherlock as does science. Both are equally as relevant to the action and scenery of the stories.

Fairie...a land that exists in parallel to Sherlock's world and through which Lord Graystone (Lord of the Jungle) came through to become part of the Baker Street Brotherhood.

Fairie is richly endowed with magical creatures and monsters, Elves, fairies, and other fun things, as well as endless realms of green Amazon like lands. Dragons. Which have played a part in several of my first stories and a few later ones.

Nicolas Tesla...a genius who has dedicated his life to upgrading the quality of life for everyone on the planet. Witty, charming, and dangerous.

Harry Houdini...swarthy, suave, into magic in every way...physical and the real thing.

Professor Challenger...very tall, built like a bear, flaming red beard and hair. Quick to temper, but a kind man with a great mind. An adventurer beyond measure.

Captain Nemo...a reformed pirate with a mind that grasps mechanics that rivals Henry Ford and Nicolas

Tesla. Is famous for his extremely powerful weapon of the sea...the Nautilus.

Jules Verne...a genius when it comes to theories and fiction, blonde, extremely friendly, caring, and adventurous. Teams up often with H.G. Wells, a friend he grew up with. Designer of the Master of the World, which in another set of Victorian adventures he uses to fight an invasion from Mars.

H.G. Wells...a brilliant writer and navigator. Contributes to the flying device Master of the World and its ability to fly through space and time. Very British and a bit stuffy at times.

Alexander Dumas...a French friend of Jules in one of the worlds I've created for Jules to explore in unique adventures that do not include H.G. Wells. Huge man with a lust for adventure and fighting.

Henry Ford...still an arrogant man, but more willing to help others, and often teams up with Tesla to do projects. Not prominent yet in my stories but working on it.

Master of the World...a huge flying machine that resembles a cross between a dirigible and a submarine that travels utilizing String theory, with an engine that converts string energy into fuel that can thrust the ship between parallel worlds, as well as back and forth in time. Created by Jules Verne, but later improved by H.G. Wells after their battle with the Martians detailed in my prior series starting with Invaders.

Lord Graystone...my version of Tarzan, but instead of being raised by apes, he was raised by a bull dragon. Highly educated and a loyal supporter of Queen Mary of Scots and husband of Lady Shareen. Sponsors numerous charities for the poor and unwanted. Champion of Fairie.

Hyde...Doctor Jekyll performs an experiment on himself that separates the evil portion of him into a unique entity. This entity is pure evil and pure energy. It can possess anyone and once having done so, become that person. Cause them to do the unthinkable to achieve its evil plans.

Doctor Jekyll...a kind, young teacher who has made a horrible miscalculation and created an abomination of himself.... Hyde! A creature that is pure evil.

Dracula...not the Bran Stoker version, but my own. Misunderstood, not eternal and drinking human blood when no other choice is possible.

Conan Doyle...the dead Sir Arthur Conan Doyle brought from our world to the alternate reality which he is reborn into, healthy and young once more. Also, an integral part of the great detective's team at times.

Baker Street Brotherhood...a team of operatives who, upon occasion, help Sherlock and Watson in their missions. Some of the more notable ones are Lord Graystone (Lord of the Jungle), Madame Curie, Dracula, Professor Langston (The Invisible Man), Professor Challenger (also a Conan Doyle character), Sir Arthur Conan Doyle himself (reborn from our world to the new one without losing awareness of himself), Lady Shareen (our equivalent of Indiana Jones), Jules Verne and H.G. Wells.

Obviously, there are many, many more, but these are the most frequently guested characters in my stories and novels.

Request for Review

If you found some pleasure in reading my work, please take the time to leave a review for it. Authors can thrive or die for the lack of reviews.

Thanking you in advance for your kindness.

John

Author's Note

If you want to keep abreast the latest news, follow me on my author site: www.bakerstreetuniverses.com

Connect with me on Twitter: @johnpirillo

Friend me at my Facebook page: John Pirillo, Author.

Join my Baker Street Universe group to get things I don't usually share with others, and to hash over the universe I've created with me and fellow authors and readers. I'll be having special giveaways, advance copies, and autographed work as well as other surprises to my friends who join me there.

The Baker Street Universe Facebook group page is a place to interact with me on a frequent basis.

My artwork is available at: https://john-pirillo.pixels.com/